THE BLACK GALLERY

ASH ERICMORE

D & T
PUBLISHING

PRAISE FOR ASH ERICMORE

"Ericmore's writing is poetic, unlike anything I've ever read before, or since."
William Shakespeare, author of *Henry V*

"Mesmerising … and unmissable. A true work of art. Deserves to be in the Louvre."
Leonardo Di Vinci, creator of *Anatomy*

"Reads like an opium hit."
Sherlock Holmes, author of *Not Now Watson, and other Limericks.*

1

"I DON'T SEE why we have to ring and book." Andrew wanted nothing to do with it. He just wanted a nice, quiet Friday night. One where he could have a drink. Sit in front of the TV. Find a DVD to watch. Be told by Janey that *DVDs were bullshit* and *why weren't they watching it on a streaming service? Because,* he would reply, *the stream services censored the movies. You just want to see more tits,* she'd rebuttal. Andrew sighed. "Okay," he said quietly.

She looked up from her coffee, a surprised eyebrow raised.

He picked up his phone and Googled the place. Rung the number. The voice at the other end sounded harassed. They didn't *need* to answer the phone—would have been easier if they hadn't to be fair—but they had. Asked what they could do for him. It was a man. "I believe I need to book an appointment, to come in and see you?" He asked. Polite as punch, in his opinion. "My wife would like to come tonight, if that's at all possible. I know it's such short notice." He glanced at Janey and it clearly wasn't lost on her that he'd added that on the end as a get-out-of-it clause.

Of course it was all right, the man said.

Fuck. He really wanted to re-watch *Starship Troopers* tonight, and *not* because of the shower scene.

How many will there be in the party?

"Two," Andrew answered. "Just myself and my wife."

The man asked if eight would be all right.

"That'll be perfect," Andrew said, teeth slightly gritted. He hung up the phone. "Eight," he said to Janey. She smiled and half nodded, getting her way as usual. Which was fine. He could watch the movie when they got home. It'd probably be too late by then for her to stay up and watch it with him, and that was okay with him. Better, in fact. Yes. Going to this place tonight was definitely for the best. "What shall I wear?" he asked her. In for a penny, in for a pound, he supposed. Funny saying that one. It really was quite different, being in for one over the other.

"How about your white t-shirt and a clean pair of jeans."

The way she said *clean* implied he usually wore dirty ones. "Fine," he said. He slid his phone down on the counter and left the kitchen, making some half-hearted attempt at gesturing that he was going to change. Then he went upstairs and pulled his trousers off, picking his jeans from the bedroom floor. He sniffed them. Nothing wrong with them. Didn't know what she was talking about.

So, he pulled them on. Took a crisp white t-shirt from the wardrobe and pulled that on too. Looked himself in the mirror. If it wasn't for the bump in the middle of his torso—his slight pot belly —he cut quite the handsome look. Then he breathed out. Although, there was very little point in it. Janey was barely interested anymore.

No. She wanted to go to a gallery. Because it looked interesting.

Fucking Friday night.

———

Andrew shovelled what felt like a thousand random coins in the slot of the parking machine and watched the time go up on the little display. He plunged his hand into his pocket and pulled out what coins were left, along with a piece of manky tissue (which for some reason he always had in his pocket, although he never used a tissue for anything), and found the last coin that he had was the one pound coin he always carried to put in the trolley at Tesco. Which he dutifully fed into the machine. A glance to Janey sitting in the passenger seat of the car, glaring at him. Then back to the coin eater. He just needed to remember that he'd done it, and get another one out of the jar when he got home. So he didn't end up at Tesco with no coin. Which he was guaranteed to do, regardless. Then he was going to have to go around Tesco with a cunting shopping basket, and it was going to get heavier and fucking heavier, and he was going to say it was all right, and *his* fault because *he* was the one who forgot the coin, because he put it in the machine in the high street, just up the hill from the poxy gallery that *she* wanted to go to.

Andrew sucked air in, getting breathless just thinking like that. Then he pressed the big green button and the grey eater of coins spewed out a little white ticket that let him stop for nearly two hours.

Fucking high street on-street parking fucking prices.

He turned back to the car and nodded, smiling at Janey like nothing had just happened. Like he hadn't just used the trolley coin for the fucking ticket machine.

He opened the driver's door and pushed the ticket on the dash. Janey sat there. Waiting. Waiting for him to go and open the door and let her out like he was ... he was ... fucking Jeeves. So, he slid around to the passenger door and opened it. Like Jeeves. She got out. Didn't even say thank you. Didn't mention his clean jeans either. Whatever.

Then the two of them stood on the path and stared at the place. It was a bit weird. Out of place. Middle of the high street. The windows—originally, windows—bricked up and painted black, the door, black. No window in that either.

"Do we knock?" Andrew said, absently.

Janey huffed a little and almost pushed him out of the way to get to the road. She crossed while he watched, and once on the other side, Andrew followed. She stood by the door and looked back at him, waiting. So, he crossed the road and went to the door. He knocked. Waited. One hand in his pocket, gently thumbing his phone, wondering if he should use that instead. Call.

The latch behind the door clacked, and the door cracked open. A man beyond. He looked dishevelled. He looked at the two of them and smiled. "Andrew," he said. Without speaking, there seemed to be some look of recognition in his eyes. He pulled the door open. Andrew glanced at Janey, a little unsure of the weirdness of the situation, before she stepped forward and entered.

Andrew shrugged. He stepped in after her.

2

"I'm Damian Hampton," the man said, turning to the young couple as he closed the door behind them. The room beyond the door was black. Every surface, matte black, painted so you couldn't see the edges, so to speak. There was a desk that neither Andrew nor Janey noticed when they first came in, camouflaged within the black. He stooped over it, a privacy shield stopping the two of them from seeing what he was looking at. "Yes," he said, "Andrew." He looked up to Andrew and gave a difficult smile, his look moving to Janey. "You must be ...?" He let the question hang.

"Janey," she answered. She grinned wildly at him, Andrew watching the infatuation grow.

Oh, here we go, he thought. Another superstar artist that we'll just *have* to buy something from and take home. It would be an investment, wouldn't it? Of course it would. He looked at Hampton. Fucking bum. He let a polite smile crawl across his face.

"Well," Hampton began, "it's only tradition, but if you'd like to go through the black door, Andrew, I will accompany your wife through the other black door and we will meet up, eventually."

Huh? "I'm sorry?" Andrew said, getting a swift elbow in the ribs from Janey. Great. She was bowled over by bullshit theatrics, and he was playing a divide-and-conquer game. Clearly. This was going to cost. He glanced at Janey, as she already was making her way to the artist, her hand out, as it slipped under his arm.

Hampton smiled at Andrew, taking his wife's hand. "The left, Andrew," he said.

Andrew looked around quickly, trying to find the black matte doors in the black matte room. And when he did, he stepped up to the left one. Janey was looking up into the artist's face like a lifelong groupie. She hadn't even seen his art yet. Andrew hoped it stank. He sucked it up and cleared his throat, curled his fingers around the handle, and opened the door. It was white beyond. A perfect white cutting through the black. Sharp. Almost blinding. He gave one last look to his wife, had a strange feeling about this … weirdness … and stepped through into the white.

The door closed behind him, Andrew turned and looked back, and there was no handle to reopen it. He frowned and looked to the direction he was supposed to go. It was a long hallway. White. The walls were smooth, but painted. Not like the kitchen, though. No. The lines in the walls were hard and thick. Like oil paints. The hallway was wide enough for there to be three mannequins on the right, room for him to walk down the left. Each mannequin had a light over it. The room was luminescent with bright white, matte, but somehow sheened still, the lights bouncing from the figures stood there. All facing the wall. They were on tiny little plinths, maybe four inches tall. Andrew stared at them for a moment, taking in a slow breath. *Great*, he thought. He hoped he wasn't going to end up taking a mannequin home. He shivered at the thought. Waking up in the middle of the night to find some tall bald thing standing in the corner, hidden by shadow, night after night.

God only knew what Janey was getting up to with Hampton. He was probably selling her a set of the fucking things.

Fucking hell.

Andrew glanced around himself one last time. Nowhere to go but forward. He guessed that at the end of the corridor there would be a white door. One that he couldn't see yet. Either that or this was the shortest fucking ride ever. The corridor felt sterile. Almost otherworldly as he strolled towards the mannequins. The whiteness of the hallway made the walk feel longer than it could have been. As he got closer, he saw that the mannequins were typical looking storefront ones. Hairless women. But naked. Very artistic. He assumed that Janey was getting a tour of something that the artist thought more in tune with her sensibilities—probably a tour of his trousers would likely work on most smitten admirers—and not this … *garbage*. It was like walking through the backrooms of Debenhams. Utter bullshit. He stopped at the first mannequin. Looked at the back of its head. It was smooth, but not quite the plastic he expected. The body was twisted, slightly, at an unnatural angle. Much like it had been discarded by Debenhams and this hack artist had installed it here without so much as a thought. Not even bothering to pose it. Andrew arched his head closer to the doll. On closer inspection, it wasn't a *shitty* mannequin. It was a quite expensive one, actually, by the looks of it, but nonetheless a fucking doll called *art*. The reason that the mannequin wasn't the colour he was expecting was because it wasn't made of shitty mannequin plastic. It looked like it was made of some sort of soft polymer. A rubber, textured material.

Then the fucking thing turned around.

Andrew stumbled back a little, his hand reaching the wall behind him as he cried out in surprise at this shit horror movie jump scare. "What?" he said. The mannequin … woman … it was a woman … stared at him. High cheekbones, almost sculpted looks, a basic line of lipstick crossing her plump lips. Her eyes on his as he steadied himself. She was perfectly formed, giving her the appearance of being cast from a mould. She was bald and naked. He glanced instinctively down her body. Her shape, that of a model. Perfectly shaped breasts that stood pert like someone from Instagram, not porn. He glanced down further. That was bald, too. *Jesus, man.* "Sorry," he blurted, unable to decide on anything better to say as he realised he was staring at her … you know. "I didn't know you were …" he stopped speaking, his brain floundering as it searched for the next word to use to finish the sentence, "… real."

She reached down with janky, mechanical motions like she was some 50s automaton, her fingers sliding between her legs, like she was going to put on a wank show for him. Andrew's confused frown lightened slightly, as she then began to stroke herself. She smiled, parting her ruby red lips, teeth smeared in red as blood poured viscous from her maw.

"Oh, God," Andrew cried, sliding on the wall away from her, slipping down towards the next. Clots of blood spewed from the woman's mouth as she groaned out in pleasure, the blood oozing thickly down her body. Andrew couldn't remove his eyes as he moved. Halfway to the second mannequin, it turned, too. She was also naked. They all were. Andrew's look moving between the first and second of them. The first with her blood drooling from her, cascading from her chin onto her perfect breasts. Blood dribbling slick down her torso. Her fingers coated in sticky blodges of blood, still between her legs, reaming slowly, in and out. "What the fuck," Andrew mouthed, silently. His eyes flicking to the second mannequin, wide in confusion and horror. She turned to him, same as the first, janky robotic movements, but she was clearly a model, an actress. Andrew, pushing himself harder against the wall, and sliding along towards her with no way to go back. His subconscious moving him forward. She was standing there. Staring. Unblinking at him. Like she wasn't alive. *They're just actors*, he thought, sliding closer, ever closer. As he moved slowly, so did her head, imperciev- ably slowly, watching him. Staring into him. And as he reached her, she suddenly jerked forward, vomiting blood out over the floor between them. Hanging her head there for a second, letting the blood slobber from her, slipping out, cold, and thick. When she straightened, her mouth drawn into a smile, filling the air with this giggle of a schoolgirl, a tease, child-like but terrifying as it echoed around them in the windowless room. Andrew cried out, "No … shit." He looked back to the door with no handle at one end of the hallway, and then to the other, praying there *was* a doorway he couldn't see. He trampled through the blood, dark stained lumps, on the stark white floor. Smearing imprints of his foot impressions as he stumbled forward. He lurched by her and the third turned. Andrew's heart hammered against his chest, palpitations raging, beats skipping like this was going to push him into having some heart attack. Was this fucking Hampton's game? Kill off the husband by forcing his art on him? Fucking *art*. His feet unconsciously moving a little quicker, he hurried towards the third, insistent in his own head that he was going to move by it, ignoring it. Try not to look at it, all the while it watched him. As he got closer, this one didn't vomit or drool blood—*it was paint*, he was telling himself, *of course it was paint*—and he stopped. He didn't mean to, couldn't help himself. He looked at her. She was facing him. Perfectly beautiful to behold, her eyes on his no matter where his were, he looked at her body, his heart slowing as he finally relaxed, and *appreciated* the art. She was shaven to the skin expertly, every inch of her body hairless; like hair had never been there to start with. Like something out of a science fiction film. He focussed down on her mound. So smooth you could *almost* mistake it for plastic, but as his eyes rose to her torso, admiring her breasts, he could see the smallest perceived movement. That of her breath. He stared at her breasts.

Then she wrenched forward, a single step, and she puked red paint over him.

Andrew staggered back, the spell she'd held over him broken, he looked down at himself. "Fuck," he screamed. He banged hard against the wall, and the unseen door at the end of the corridor opened. The lights in this hallway extinguished, all but the bar light over the door, and he could barely make out the women, plunged into a nightmare blackness. He wiped his hands down, through the liquid the third one had spat over him. Raised his hand to his nose and sniffed. The liquid was thick, sticky, but he was sure it was paint, even though there was a copper smell to it, something that he didn't recognise. He shook his head and stepped into the light and through the door.

Into the darkness beyond.

The door closed behind him. Automated. And he was suddenly plunged into a void of dark, the light from above the door on the other side, gone. He pushed his hand out to steady himself, seeking a wall. "Hampton," he called out. "Enough of this. You're getting my dry cleaning bill."

There was no echo of his voice, like he was in a sound chamber or something, some room, perfectly soundproofed. "Fucking people," he muttered. "They think because they're a so-called *artist* they can get away with anything." He started waving his hand out in front of him. The room was painted in perfect black. "Well," he huffed. "Someone's got another thing coming." His voice rose in volume. "If you've … upset my wife," he shouted, "then you have no idea what I have in store for you." Yes. That was a threat, wasn't it? Threaten him with Janey next. Really scare the shit out of him.

There was an audible clunk. The lights came on.

The room was red. Matte, the same as everything else in this godforsaken place, except this time the walls themselves looked to be painted in clotting oils. There was no door, at least that he could see, apart from the one he'd come in through—again handle-less, stopping his retreat. Not that he wanted to go back that way, particularly. He spun in a slow circle, trying to find the exit, his focus on the walls, before concentrating on anything else in the room. He wanted out, *now*. In the light, he glanced down at his jeans, stained from the paint, now black looking, mixed with the denim.

White t-shirt, fucked.

Then he looked at what was in the centre of the room.

Freestanding. At first, he thought it was an exercise machine. There was a figure—looked like a mannequin—on it. It was a tall structure, black brushed metal, perhaps, and the woman—of course —was laying at forty-five degrees. She was naked. This guy was a real fucking pervert. Her hands up, above her head, bound. Her legs parted.

Andrew came around in front of the device and looked up at the … mannequin. It looked like the women in the previous hallway, but this one had to be a doll of some sort. They did miracle things with sex dolls these days, didn't they? He'd seen them on the internet. Very lifelike.

It was a torture device of some sort, something modernised but medieval, all at the same time. The figure, tied down, spread eagle, naked. She was cut open, her guts spilled out down her. Dried blood over her. That was how he knew she was a mannequin. He could see *inside* her. She was deathly pale, a neat paint job, for sure. And there was another part—part of the modernisation of the device, Andrew considered. A fucking machine. Some extension of the device between her legs, inserted inside her. A long rod, simulating a long, metallic penis. The room smelt bad, too. And everything felt sticky. Like there was moisture in the air.

And as he stood there, watching. The machine started. Slowly. The sound of hydraulics pulling back the shaft between her legs, drawing it forward, and then the hiss as it pushed it back inside her. Fucking this … thing. Andrew felt a little sick, but he couldn't look away. "What kind of *installation* is this?" he shouted into the void, unable to avert his eyes.

The machine increased in speed. Fucking the mannequin. Andrew couldn't help but step closer, his sickening feeling overrun by intrigue. The *dick* end was slathered in blood—paint, he corrected himself, *paint*—sticky to look at, as it pulled the remarkably realistic skin of the mannequin's violated vagina back and forth with its movement. Andrew leant in. The mannequin stank like a butcher shop. He looked into the gap that was this *woman's* torso, through the intestines, through to the guts, stomach, and he could see the dick end pushing the organs about. Jabbing itself into the stomach, flexing it like a set of bagpipes.

All very realistic, he thought. He looked down closer at the vagina. You know, out of interest. Then the mannequin screamed. The thing pushed itself up and bellowed out at Andrew. He stumbled back, away from the contraption and fell, splayed on the floor. "Fucking hell," he cried. He rolled over, his elbow hurt. Someone was getting sued for this. He pushed his way back to his feet and turned back to the fucking machine, still fucking. The simulation penis rocking back and forth, deep into the woman, laying back like it had never moved. *What the fuck?* He stepped back over, massaging his elbow. Prepared now for more noise and shouting and shit. But then the machine began to slow, and the fucking deceased in speed. Andrew stood there, within reach. His hand moving forward, almost subconsciously. He was trembling. Couldn't help it. But he had to know. He had to touch the ... mannequin. Feel it *cold*. If it was cold, it was art, right? Plastic. Non ... human. Because that was what all this was. A trick. Smoke and mirrors. He told himself that, and it made him feel better. Yes. It's parlour tricks. But the lights extinguished in the room, plunging Andrew back into the perfect dark, before he reached its skin. The skin he knew would be cold.

A door opened, illuminated in the darkness.

Andrew was left standing there, looking at it. He suddenly felt rather silly, so he dropped his hand, unable to clearly see what he was reaching for any longer, and so it all felt like it was art. It *had* to be art. A short breath in through his nose and he could smell shit. It was him; he was sure. He'd wet farted, hopefully. Andrew turned back to the door, to the light, and hurried over to it. Out into the next room.

White.

The walls matte. Nothing in it.

The door behind him closed, and he stood there. Slightly stunned by it all. He didn't even look behind him, knowing that the door that had just closed would have no handle.

But there was a door on the other side of the white room. He walked to it. His legs jellied. His stomach had butterflies swimming about inside. He really had no idea what to think about all that *art*. A room full of monkeys could make better art than that. That much he did know. Whatever that was, it wasn't Van fucking Gogh, that was for sure. Fucking exploitation art. Some millennial joke. Well, at least it didn't cost anything to come here. That was something. And God only knew what Janey was going to think of it all. Christ. He blinked, reaching the door.

He'd only been in there a few minutes. How much more of this was there? Hopefully not a lot, and he'd have more time to drink. He needed a drink.

The door in front of him opened by itself, swinging away from him, beyond … a carpeted floor. Black and grey. He stepped through and there was a wing-backed armchair in the centre of the room. A small coffee table stood next to it. The room was decked out in warm golds and reds, starkly different to the previous rooms. He stumbled, stunned, into the room and went to the chair, looking around. No visible exits—no surprise there. The door behind him had closed, of course—not that he was intending to go back that way—and so he sat.

"Fuck this bullshit," he muttered. He looked down at his stained clothing. He looked like he'd fucking murdered someone. "Hello?" he called. There was a drink in a mug on the coffee table. His, he assumed. Or maybe part of the art. He'd given up trying to understand all this. So, he picked up the mug, steaming, and smelled it. Wouldn't be surprised if it was fucking poison. Jesus. This fucking place.

The drink smelled of mince pie. Odd. But something of a luxury item you could normally only get at Christmas in coffee shops. He sipped it. It was perfect.

Weirdly perfect.

His Christmassy embrace was interrupted by a light hissing sound, and a door opposite the chair opened. Unseen, blended perfectly into the walls, it came from the floor like something out of Star Trek. He watched it. Squinting. Surprisingly exhausted after visiting the *exhibits*. There was someone behind the door. It must cost Hampton a fortune to hire all these actors to pretend to be art for him, probably getting cleaned up between performances.

The door opened fully, and behind it was a woman. At first, because of her lack of movement, Andrew guessed it might be another mannequin, but was certainly going to assume nothing at this point. But after a moment's pregnant pause, she stepped from the shadows of the door. She was naked, painted with a fascinating mural of oiled landscape, something wildly beautiful, covering every inch of her body. She had long, flowing blond hair. Beauty that was unaccountable. She strode to him, moving like a ballet dancer, fluid movements of poise and grace. Stopping only when she reached the side of the chair. Andrew stared up at her, his mince pie coffee an inch from his lips.

"Fucking hell," he said.

His eyes danced down her, taking in both the woman and the painting. Underneath the oil was the most stunning woman he thought he'd ever seen. She was impeccable under his eye, every fantasy woman he'd ever thought of smooshed together into this body, and the oils on top, a cascading art work of beauty and style. The collected works of Monet and Turner and Constable paling in comparison.

He sipped his coffee, unable to remove his eyes from her.

Then she moved, swaying just slightly as she pushed her fingers into the oil and started to change it. So carefully, like the artist themselves, applying it to start with. Andrew watched as the oil paint moved around itself, melting and moulding and melding, creating new and fantastic images, drawing and re-drawing the picture on her skin, the destruction of one beauty, the creation of another. His mouth, agape, he watched as she slowly redrew, again, and again, until all he could see was the myriad of colours, never before seen, his eyes wide and unblinking. She leant forward, her hand wrapping around his cock, as he realised he was hard, and he squirmed away, embarrassed. "Oh, God," he said, "I am so sorry ..." he pushed himself deep into the chair, as the art stroked him through his jeans. He wanted it to stop ... but he didn't. "No," he whispered, staring into the beauty. She smiled under the colours, the picture, the nothing that was now everything. Her fingers were tight, stroking him closer to orgasm.

She stopped, released him. "But you must come back," she whispered. Her voice was silken caramel. He lusted after the touch, and now the sound of her voice. He had to have ... and then she returned to the door. Naked, painted. Perfect. His mouth open. The coffee still steaming his face. He watched her disappear behind the closing door.

Gone.

Then the lights in the room came up.

Everything suddenly feeling cold and sterile. He sipped his coffee and crossed his legs, waiting for his raging boner to just hurry up and fuck off. What the fuck was that? What had gotten into him? His body relaxing, he finished his drink before moving from the chair and going to the door out, visible once the lights had risen.

The door opened before him and he stepped out into the warm black of the reception room he'd been in before. There, on a black sofa, were Janey and Hampton.

3

"Isn't it wonderful?" she said. She looked from Andrew to Hampton. Her eyes wide and he could see she was utterly enthralled by him.

"What?" Andrew said. He wiggled his hips uncomfortably, having lost his erection only moments before.

"That Mr. Hampton wants to *do* me."

"Damian," Hampton corrected her.

"Damian," she said wistfully.

"What?" Andrew blurted. That didn't seem right. Not after what he'd seen.

"I'd like to paint your wife," Hampton said. "She's quite lovely."

Andrew shook his head, immediately thinking of the *art* in the final room. Then the installation in the one before that. The fucking. All the women. The nakedness. Blood. Goo. Erections. No. No, she had no idea what was behind door number one. "No," Andrew said, like he had been asked a question.

Hampton smiled, a gesture not shared by Janey. She snapped her head towards him, tearing it from the artist where it had been, all kissy face and whatnot. Now she was frowning. Actually, she looked rather like thunder incarnate. "What?" The way she said it, it was enough to know that he would not win this argument he'd just started without a very good reason.

"No," Andrew said, his brain whirring like it had a hamster on crack in there, going at the wheel like it was the last wheel on earth. "I've seen … Mr. Hampton's installations. His *art*. I don't think he wants to *do you* in the same fashion that I think you want to be done." He was rambling and this was making no sense to him, let alone her. "I mean I saw the naked women," he said, pointing to the door he went into originally. "And the one on the fucking machine. And then that last one touched me." His finger pointing had moved from the *in* door to the *out* door, and then, even though the words had spilled from his mouth without thought, Andrew did shut up, considering that he had, perhaps, just made this worse. She was frowning again, and Andrew knew his argument was flawed. In more ways than one. With the whole *your art touched me* argument. It was a losing battle on more than one front. If he could persuade her that Hampton was going to want her to strip naked and give out handies, then he'd still have to explain that Hampton's art had stripped naked.

And given out a handy.

He wasn't sure if he wanted a doll to point at, either. The still quiet in the room was exacerbated by the loudest thing in the room being Andrew's excitable breathing. It was suddenly very warm in there.

"They aren't women, Andrew," Hampton cut through the silence. "They are art."

Gesturing at the art smeared down his clothing, Andrew replied, "You can call them what you will, but you're not doing that to my wife." He held his hand out for Janey to take so he could pull her from the sofa, and they could leave. United. Together.

She ignored him.

"You wife is perhaps the most stunning creature in all of God's creation, Andrew. You, the luckiest man in all the world, should share nothing but the image of this creation. I ask for nothing but to take what your wife has and recreate it."

"Like those women out there?" Andrew was pointing again. And gobsmacked. Pointing and gobsmacked. What was this ... cretin ... trying to say? That this silly talk made it okay? That he *objectified* them?

"They are not women," he said, again. "Mannequins," he continued. "They are effigies."

Andrew shook his head. "That last one. That was a *woman*." He glanced from Hampton to Janey. "She touched me. Inappropriately. I know she was a woman."

Janey was staring at him. He was in trouble now. She'd want details. Maybe later, but she'd want them. Want to know what he'd been up to behind closed doors, even though it was her idea to go there. But once she saw sense, it was all going to be worth it. She'd forgive him. He'd save her from the inappropriateness that this so-called *artist* was going to put her through.

"You *are* mistaken." Hampton smiled. There was something behind his calmness. Something dark that frightened Andrew.

"We should go," he said again. He still had his hand out.

"We should," Janey said. She pushed herself to stand without taking his hand. "But I do want to return, Mr. Ha ... Damian. Please. I want you to turn me into whatever art you see fit." She glanced at Andrew before the look dropped away. It was pity.

Andrew was shaking his head. Let his hand drop.

"Perhaps my husband will find such exhilaration in that which you do to me, that he has found in the other works you have here."

Hampton smiled at Andrew. "Perhaps."

———

"So, what did he show you?" Andrew said, starting the engine. Trying to remain composed while he waited for the tempest that was boiling just below the surface of his wife. "Because I *clearly* saw something quite different."

"Clearly." Janey stared out the window. She spoke in *that* tone. The one where Andrew knew he was in trouble, but she wasn't just going to have it out with him. Not yet. "Stop at a drive thru. I want something to eat."

Yes dear. Andrew drove around the block and out onto the main road towards the local Maccies. They drove in silence for a few minutes. Which was good, because Andrew was fuming and didn't want to say something that he'd later regret. Like some woman had fondled him behind closed doors.

"I gave him our phone number," she said, cutting through the fog of war laying in the car.

"Oh." Andrew said.

"So he'll call in a few days."

"What do you want?"

"I'd like an oil. Something sexy, maybe for the bedroom."

Andrew shot her a look. "From the drive thru," he clarified.

"Oh. Triple."

Andrew pulled up to the old broken down voice machine. It asked what he wanted and he ordered the burger. Nothing for himself. He didn't have an appetite. Why the fuck couldn't she just listen to him? "I think he's a fucking psycho," he said, pulling from the voice machine to the queue. *Yes.* That was going to steer the conversation in the right direction. He pulled around the corner, slow, bumper to bumper, to the window and took the bag he was given. Thrust it at her. She took it. Silently. Unwrapped the burger. He listened to her chewing. Loudly. Andrew huffed and stared out at the traffic. Heavy for that time of night. He drew the car out onto the road towards the roundabout. Maybe if he just steered the car into the oncoming traffic, he could sleep in a hospital bed tonight.

Probably going to be more comfortable than the sofa.

4

———————

Andrew dreamt of the backrooms of the Black Gallery. The White Hallway with the women, bloodied. The Red Room with the fucking machine. The art touching him. Wanting him to return. He opened his eyes. Nearly shit when he found Janey standing over him. "Fuck," he blurted. "What?"

She was staring down at him, smiling.

"Damian called."

Shit. That had happened like three days ago. He was hoping she'd have forgotten all about it. Or at least that whacko artist would have. "And what did he have to say for himself?" Andrew pushed himself up onto his elbow and squinted in the daylight. What time was it?

"He's invited us in to meet with him. He wants to clear the air, and get your agreement to do me."

He wished she'd stop phrasing it like that.

"He's the most understanding of gentlemen. Even when dealing with *you*." She smiled again.

"I don't want to." Andrew collapsed back onto the bed.

"We're meeting him at three, at the gallery."

Of course we are. Andrew smiled at her, and she turned and left the bedroom. Right. Fine.

"We can go to Tesco on the way," she called from the landing.

Great. Shopping too. Andrew loved shopping.

5

JANEY KNOCKED on the door of the gallery. Waiting patiently. Andrew was looking skyward, completely convinced that no matter what was said in the meet, that he would not change his stance on allowing Janey to be *done*. Not that it really mattered, did it? His opinion was moot in her mind, of course, and to be honest, the fact that Hampton wanted to speak with him said more about the artist than it did anything else.

The door opened, and Hampton ushered them in. "Good morning," he said.

"Afternoon," Andrew corrected, getting a glare from the wife. "Good morning," he continued, looking away from her.

Hampton went straight to the left door, to the beginning of Andrew's journey through the installations. "I think we need to clarify a few things, before I take your wife … under my wing, so to speak."

"Yes," Andrew said. This was it. He was going to show Janey all the women. And he was going to be reprieved. Apart from the nakedness. She wasn't going to like that. Not one little bit. But it was give and take. He would be given the benefit of the doubt, and she would refuse the offer from Hampton. Then she would take his balls and keep them in her handbag forever. Exchange is no robbery.

Hampton led them through into the white corridor. The three women stood in the same places as before. He took them along the corridor to the first and just as they approached, the janky movement began and the mannequin turned, moved by a turntable built into the floor. It rotated and faced them. Dead eyed and plastic-y. "You see," Hampton said. "Just a dummy."

Andrew wasn't going to get played for a dummy. This was different. He leaned into the face of the mannequin—clearly a mannequin. "No," he said, matter-of-factly. "The ones in here the other day were breathing."

"I can assure you not." Hampton seemed to look embarrassingly to Janey, with apparent concern for Andrew's mental health.

Andrew raised his fingers to the mannequin's face. He was going to touch it. He wanted to know if the material that this thing was made of was pliable enough to be what he … no. This mannequin was made of hard plastic. He didn't need to touch it. He could clearly see. There was absolutely no way this was the same thing. Hampton was lying. "I don't think so," Andrew said, quietly.

"So, it's settled," said Janey. "We can continue."

Andrew looked from the mannequin to Janey. Then to Hampton. "It touched me," he said.

Hampton shook his head. "No." He reached up and gently took Andrew's hand. "Please don't touch. They are very expensive."

Andrew frowned. This was a lie. This artist had changed them. He'd had actors in here for the performance and put these here as a smoke screen. "No," Andrew said. Defiant. "The next room." The fucking machine that was fucking a cut up woman. He strode with purpose towards the door at the end, and when it didn't open for him, he turned back to Hampton and Janey and snapped his fingers together. "Stop stalling," he said. "Open up."

Hampton caught up to him, followed by Janey. She looked more pitifully at him now, rather than angry. Hampton fiddled with what looked like a remote and the door behind Andrew opened out into the red room and Andrew strode in. "Look," he said, pointing at the machine in the centre of the room. Lit, he strode to it. Clear as day, it was a mannequin on a medieval rack.

"It's just lighting and mechanics," Hampton said, turning his attention to Janey. "I really *am* so sorry about this."

Janey shook her head. "It is I that must apologise for my husband's behaviour. I do hope it won't affect our discussions about you doing me."

"Of course not," Hampton said. He rested his hand on her shoulder. Like he was consoling her.

For Andrew's behaviour.

Andrew was staring at the rack. It was a fucking lie. All of it. This wasn't what was here. At all. *None of it*. He shook his head and headed to the next door. Pushed it open himself this time, shoving it. Into the small empty room. He wasn't having this fucking artist make a monkey out of him. He strode across to the next door, pushing that one, too. The door opened, and the room beyond that was also empty. "No," he said. "There was a chair behind this door —" he pointed at the door the painted lady had come from, "—her, she came from there." Janey was looking at him like he was an abomination. Making this shit up because he was what? Jealous? Fucking hell. Fuck that. He shook his head. "Whatever," Andrew snapped. "Do what you want."

"I can assure you," Hampton said, joining Janey in the doorway. "That my intentions are perfectly admirable."

Andrew shrugged. "Yeah," he said quietly.

Hampton led them through the final door back to the reception area. Andrew looked around as he moved, looking for signs that what he had said was true, but what could he possibly find that would prove it? Blood stains? Red stains in an artist's space. *Shit.* Hampton walked to the sofa and gestured for the two of them to sit.

"How about …" he smiled, "… why don't you come when your wife does? You can ensure her safety from the *mad artist*." His smile widened, while Janey turned crimson. She shot Andrew a glance, and he could see her begging him not to agree.

"That would be ideal," he said, quietly. "Thank you."

"Then it is settled," Hampton said, his voice louder, like he had *won* something. "Please, would Saturday be a possibility?" He rounded the desk and started to look through his diary. "I don't have any appointments that day. I could do a sitting all day." His eyes rose to Janey. "The sittings are long, and a little of a challenge if you are not used to them. I can break up the time. You'll be tortured if we have the whole day." His smile warmed. "I'm sure we can find something for you to do, too, Andrew."

Andrew nodded. Yes. That would do.

6

"I DON'T KNOW what to wear," Janey said, faffing through the wardrobe. Andrew glanced over at her.

He was sitting on the bed, the broadsheet open, tiring his arms, while he stared blankly at the words, swimming together, thinking about the film that was on TV last night. Or at least some of the film. Okay. The naughty bits. "I don't want you to go," he said. And not for the first time.

"I'm going to be immortalised," she said, ignoring him.

Yeah, he thought. *Immortalised*. Fucking balls. Hampton was a bell-end and if he thought he could have gotten away with it, he'd have dropped into the gallery last night on the way home from work and cancelled the appointment. With his foot. Up Hampton's arse. "You don't know what I saw." He flipped the newspaper down and looked over the top of it. She was standing, looking into the wardrobe, her chin in her cupped hand. In her underwear. Black. Silky stuff. Sexy. Sort of stuff she should be keeping aside for him. Not some fucking weirdo with an art studio and a bunch of half-naked chicks covered in paint and blood.

She huffed out a sigh. "Whatever," she whispered.

Andrew wasn't sure if he was supposed to have heard it or not.

"You think he'll want me nude?"

Andrew raised the paper back up nodding to himself. *Oh, very much so.* But he wasn't about to let the madman turn her into the same installation that he saw last week. Oh no. She might not appreciate him now, but when she realised he'd stopped her from being hoisted and lain bare on a fucking machine, her guts in the corner of the room … well, then she'd appreciate him. He glanced around the paper. *Poor Janey*, he thought. Just wants an oil or something. No. He would go and protect her from this foul artist. Then she'd appreciate him. "Probably have you giving handies to patrons if you ask me." He heard her scoff. He probably shouldn't have said that, but fuck it.

"Whatever," she barked, before continuing to get ready.

Andrew cast the paper aside on to the bed. "Seriously," he said. "Look, I'll get you painted somewhere else. How about that? I'll take a day off work and we'll zip on to Ashbury. I'll even buy you lunch."

"I don't want to be painted somewhere else." She didn't look at him. "Or *by* someone else."

"You don't know what he's like," Andrew snapped, staring at the back of her head. He was sure she had eyes there. The number of times she'd caught him—

She turned, and the look on her face said it all. This wasn't a fight that Andrew was going to win. In fact, should he pursue it, there was a good probability that he'd need to visit the Accident and Emergency. He raised his eyebrows and sat back. Trying to be as passive as possible. He closed his eyes, listening to her, back in the wardrobe again. He wondered what would happen if he just let her get on with it. He supposed she'd trolley off and never come back. Lost to the wiles of this great artist and molesting visiting art lovers. He could go and see her. See the installation she had become. Maybe get a handjob from her. More than he was likely to get now. He snorted.

It was involuntary.

"What?" she said.

He opened his eyes and looked at her. "Nothing," he said. "Just thinking."

"I'm going. I'm going on my own. And there is nothing you can do about it. I want Damian to *do* me."

"I'll bet you do," Andrew barked. He flung his feet from the bed and stormed from the bedroom. Stupid woman. He slammed the door to be sure to punctuate his feelings. Why didn't she listen? She never did, that was why.

Christ.

Andrew stomped to the kitchen.

Slammed that door too. Opened the fridge and stared at the cold brewskis sitting in there. Teasing him. He stared at them and listened to her stamping her feet above his head. Stupid thin ceiling. He wanted the beer. The beer wanted him. He looked at the clock above the back door—the one her mother had brought them for Christmas. Stupid clock. It wasn't even time for elevenses yet.

The bedroom door slammed upstairs.

She was probably streaking down the stairs, naked, going to threaten to go like that. Well. You know what? He was going to let her. Dare her to, even.

Then the front door went.

Well.

Andrew opened the kitchen door and went to the hallway. Looked through the chink of non-frosted glass in the front door, the bit surrounded by frosted glass. The bit he glared out of when waiting for his takeaway to be delivered.

She was already in the car. Not naked. The fucking cheek of it. Engine started. Right. Well, if she wanted to become a handmaiden for some looney fucking artsy-fartsy twat, then so be it. He could redecorate the house how *he* wanted now. Yes.

He looked at the walls in the hallway. Fucking terracotta. That was going. Now that *he* was in charge. Deep red. No. Fucking *black*. His gaze returned to the front door. Heart heavier. Who was going to stop him from making incomprehensibly stupid decisions now if she never returned?

Fucking hell.

Andrew took his coat and swung it over his shoulders. "I'm coming," he said, pulling the front door open. He pulled his phone from his pocket and jabbed flaccidly at the screen trying to get his password in. "Fucking hell, Janey," he huffed, realising how out of breath he was. "Fucking stupid—"

The phone accepted his password. He thumbed in the easiest cab company number he could remember, reaching the end of the road.

"Chauffeur Taxis," the woman on the other end *spouted*.

"I need a taxi, urgently," he huffed.

"Where from?"

"Um," Andrew glanced around. "St. Richmonds Street."

"What number?"

"Twenty. Twenty-two … twenty-four." His lungs were bursting in agonising pain, feeling like he'd smoked forty fags yesterday. Hadn't smoked in years. He stopped running. "Yeah," he said. "Twenty-four."

"Be fifteen minutes," she said.

"Please hurry," he said. "My wife's in danger."

7

ANDREW DUG IN HIS WALLET, prying out a twenty. Fuck it. Cab drivers didn't like big notes for short journeys. The cab turned into the high street.

"Where do you want, mate?" he asked.

"Down the bottom," he said. Twenty quid. He was going to make sure Janey knew he'd dropped a twenty coming to rescue her from this weirdo. The taxi pulled up, and Andrew hurled his twenty over the seat, mumbling something about keeping the change.

That was Friday night's takeaway down the Swanny.

He pushed himself out of the car, checked the road, and hurried across to the blackened door of the gallery. His hand slapping on the door, open palmed. "Oi," he shouted, more than aware than people were *looking*. "*Hampton.*"

The door swung open, and Hampton looked a little pissed.

Good.

Andrew barked, "Where's my wife?" as he pushed his way past the man into the reception. The room, of course, was empty. "What have you done with her?" he asked accusingly, jabbing his finger in the man's direction.

"Nothing at all." He spoke with a serene quietness. Pleasant and polite. "I've just taken her avatar and placed it on canvas."

Andrew made a *pfft*, sound. She couldn't have been there more than fifteen minutes. Twenty at the most. Andrew ran his hand over his forehead, sweaty from the short run at the house. He really needed to get down to the gym. Or find out where there was a gym. That would be a start. Look ... if she didn't appreciate this ... "Where?" he scowled.

Hampton shrugged, pointing at one of the so far unexplored black doors in the black room. "My studio," he said.

Andrew strode to the door, fumbling for the matte handle that he could barely register in the ... blackness of everything ... and almost shouldered his way through into the studio.

The room was a strange colour, a sort of yellowed white ... the colour of bad teeth, or cum. The walls adorned with curtains, shades of white, pale offs. It was brightly lit, like opening a door out into the clouds. In the centre of the room was an artist's canvas atop an easel. Paint on it.

But no Janey.

"Where is she?" he shouted, glancing over his shoulder to Hampton, who was following him slowly from the reception to the studio.

"Taking a break," he said. "It's very tiring." He shook his head. "I did warn you both."

Andrew snorted again. "She's only just got here, you fucking fruitcake."

Hampton frowned. "I assure you not." His frown turned upside down. "Come, see what we have achieved." He stepped across Andrew and gently took his arm, leading him to the middle of the room, the canvas.

A painting of Janey.

She was naked, staring, full of desire to the artist, the paint shimmering in the warm light of the studio. He looked over it, quickly at first. Sure. Anyone can paint someone's face on a nude. From memory, even. Had she even seen this? He looked down her body, her hand gently held to the side of her mound. As if she was about to touch herself. Like she used to.

While he watched.

His cock twitched in his trousers, snapping him from the thought. No time for that, old chap. But his eyes stayed on the painting, he stared at her body. It *was* her. Every curve was hers; every inch of flesh was hers, taken from his own mind's eye and placed to the canvas, wet in oil. His fingers reached out of their own accord, wanting to touch the mound before she did.

The sound of a thousand trains passing the room filled his ears, taking his thought, the world outside becoming nothing more than an inconvenience in his desire to touch Janey. *His* Janey. "How?" he muttered. Or thought he did. He couldn't hear his own voice over the whoosh of the water drowning him. The sound of the trains. His senses dulled. How? How could she have been here long enough to have been done already? How could this fucktard know what she looked like in the nude?

Hampton pulled him by his wrist, stopping Andrew from touching the painting. "Please, don't touch." He smiled. "She's still wet."

Andrew snapped from his journey and looked at the man. "I'll bet she is," he said, pulling his hand free. "Where is she? We're going home." He looked at the painting. "I don't know how you've done this …" he let the words drift off, away, before he turned in a circle. There were no other doors in the studio. He stormed to the reception and out, looking around. There had to be changing rooms or something. This place was so … dank. He strode to the first door he saw and twisted the handle, pushing it open. The white corridor beyond.

8

"IT IS all of want and desire," Hampton cackled as Andrew weaved into the corridor. "Satiating the beast, some might say."

Andrew twisted as the corridor undulated and turned like it was the centre of a gyroscope, the three mannequins beckoning him forward, naked, perfect. Nausea spun his gut, turning his breakfast over. The three of them, moaning in pleasure, the corridor full of heat and sex. He knew there was a doorway at the other end, and this, this *trick* was just to stop him, so he pushed forward, the first of the mannequins clawing at his clothing, trying to pull his belt open.

"I'm not falling for this bullshit," he exclaimed as the dolls tried to strip him, leaving their spots, coming to him, touching him. Angry, Andrew lashed out, pushing the first back hard against the wall, but it didn't seem to stop her, groans of delight as she was gratified by his touch, no matter what it was. The three of them calling out like he was some Fabioesque lover in a cheap fuck flick. "Get away," he snapped, pushing another of the temptresses to the side. "Janey," he hollered. "I'm coming."

"Ohh," one of them giggled, "Please." Her hands over his cock, snaking around him, pulling his fly open.

"Fuck off," he said, raising his hand, and slapping her hard, knocking her back. She lost her footing, tumbling to the floor.

A sudden pang of guilt rose in Andrew, striking a woman like that. He paused, looking down on her, with suddenly nothing else mattering.

But she simply oozed more pleasure, one hand caressing the red patch on her face, the other winding in between her legs as they parted, finding her cunt moist and wanton. "Master," she moaned, "Oh, master, teach me," she whined. "Show me how to behave."

Andrew snapped his look from her and shouldered his way into the other two, through to the other side. He pulled his zipper back up and pushed his shirt back into his trousers. "Foul whores," he said, determined to make it to the end of the corridor as it writhed like some impossible snake. His stomach rolling over and over, vile, burning juices pushing their way up his throat. He tasted the machination of breakfast in his gullet as it tried to make its way to his mouth, the corridor rolling like the sea. "Fuck," he muttered, losing his footing as he turned to glance back to the mannequin women, the world turning on a spit. Crashing to the floor he scrambled along, the door—the end of the corridor—seeming to get further away the harder he pushed.

Then he was there, crashing his face into the white door as he crawled, desperate, on the floor. His hand weaving up the door like a drunk, home, early hours on Saturday morning. All he could think about was his wife. His fingers trying to find a handle that wasn't there, clawing at the smooth surface, before suddenly, the door opened.

He poured into the next room, his whole body like jelly.

He slipped in, scrabbling on the floor, pushing himself away from them … from that *fucking artist*. Andrew kicked at the door, aiding it to close, even though it was closing by itself. Andrew dropped back onto his elbows, breathing hard, the sweat running down him in floods, clothes sticking to him. Stinging his eyes as it dribbled from his lids. "Jesus … Christ," he muttered. He turned. The red room.

The fucking machine in the centre, still. Unmoving in the thick, wet feel of the room. Andrew pushed himself to his knees, then to his feet. Staring at the abomination strapped to the machine. Knowing—*knowing*—that he was going to see what he saw the first time he was here. His breathing, laboured by the stress, suddenly quietened as he watched the thing. Writhing on the machine, the machine itself, dead. He realised his hands were shaking. He wanted Janey, but he was *afraid*. He didn't want to admit it. Didn't want to be. But he was. He was unsure of what it was he was afraid of, though. The man? The machines? These ... things? As he watched, the living mannequin brought its head up, looking at him. As real as he. She mouthed the word, *please*, before dropping her head back, and the machine started.

The long, hard cylinder inside her, moving back and forth, pushing her oh so visible guts around as it probed far too deep to be anything other than a device of torture ... Andrew brought his hand up over his mouth, unable to stop the vomit, running hard and fast from his maw, through his fingers and down onto his clothes, spattering into a puddle on the floor at his feet.

The woman's guts tangling on the proboscis fucking her, yanking her insides apart, blood cascading from her, pooling on the machine, over the rim, down to the floor below, spreading into his puke, Andrew stepping back to stop her red from reaching his shoes.

He realised he was crying.

Andrew staggered away from this monstrous atrocity to the wall. Back against it, he slid along, his fingers feeling for the next door. The next room. The smell raping his nose, his head swinging around, brain swimming, the horror stamping out any rational thought he might have had.

His fingers found the door, and he pushed up against it. It opened like it knew he was there, waiting, happy to have him inside it.

Into the empty room. It spun. Sickness clawing at his stomach wall, he stumbled to the next door, watching the door to the red room close. Then the door forwards open.

He was through the door, yanking it shut as he fell back into the next room, the chair, the table. The mince pie coffee. The room was free of abominations, as he sat, collapsed on the floor, breathing so very hard. "God," he muttered, struggling to his feet, his eyes darting from the door, to the chair, to the other door. Every fibre of his wont, needing to leave. Run. Flee, it was telling him.

"Janey," he said. Crawling to his knees. Standing. His hand steadying himself on the back of the chair, the smell of the coffee invading his nose, taking the dreadful thoughts of blood and gore, breaking his thoughts, calming. Relaxing.

Normal.

He watched as the door opened from the floor. The unseen one. The one he should have been expecting. His fingers digging into the soft back of the chair, his knuckles whitening. His head involuntarily rocking from side to side. *No*, his head was telling him. *That's enough old chap.*

Beyond the door, the woman stood. Perfect in every way. Repainted to a glorious depiction of somewhere never before seen. Blacks and reds, stark against the burning white of an alien sun, resting in the sky of her breast, clouds in the colour she was last painted in, indescribable in both beauty and horror within a landscape of rotten pain. She stepped forward, beckoning him to her, her fingers finding her paint, and changing the backdrop to alien worlds having Hell rain down on them. Destruction and fire. Hate. Anger. She morphed from perfect beauty to remorse filled dirt, there before his eyes, as the painting changed, so did the heat in the room. Rising like the fires of Hell itself.

Andrew turned and ran to the door, wanting out. His fingers clawing at the edges of the door without a handle, struggling like a child desperate to open the pill bottle, eventually finding that click and then him, the pills, spilling out, into the reception room. Matte black. The smell of nothing. Hampton sitting on the sofa, a glass of brown liquid in a cut crystal tumbler in his hand, as he waited for Andrew to return.

Andrew stood, looking back at the door. Closed. Gone in the darkness of the room. A glance to Hampton. "I want my wife. I want to take her home."

9

"YOU ARE HOME," Hampton replied, his lips touching the glass, the flavour of the liquid causing a slight tick in his look. "You are home," he echoed, his words as tender as baby flesh ... quiet, warm. Welcoming.

"Where's Janey?"

Hampton pointed. "Where she always has been."

Andrew followed the line of his finger to the studio, the room he was in before. "She's *not* in there," he whispered.

"Oh, but she is," Hampton insisted.

Andrew walked to the door. His fingers on the handle. He knew Hampton was lying. He *knew* it. But he had to prove it to himself. And then what? What would he do when the room was empty? He would turn on Hampton. The man was old. A trickster. After something. He didn't know what. He didn't care much at that stage. He would just be happy to take his wife's hand and pull her from this madness. Take her home.

Love her like she deserved to be loved. Fuck it. Do anything else she ever wanted, as long as it was far from this abomination.

He took the handle of the door and pushed it open.

Beyond was the paint.

Filling the room was a convulsing image, thick, driven oil paint in shapes indescribable, pulsating to a heartbeat. There was an opening, as big as a man, dark, cavernous, drawing him forward to its pink, slick walls. A doorway in the oil. Andrew looked at it. He filled with horror and subjugation at the visage, unable to stop himself from taking the first step into the room.

The door closed behind him, quiet and gentle. And as he unconsciously reached forward, from the opening came the smell of heat. Sex. Desire and want rolled together as he stepped to the cave in the room, gaping, wide. His hand reaching forward and touching the skin of the oil. Warm. Inviting. Wet. He caressed the opening, a single glance back to the door. His erection, now private.

"Janey," he said, absently. Some recognition in him, but even he didn't know where from. "We need to leave."

But she drew him forward.

He looked up at the ceiling disappearing far into the distance. The canvas trailing the paint to nothing as he took a step inside the hole. Yawning open. Waiting for him to satiate its need for him, as he disappeared inside, the moist cavern, slippery.

His footing was unsure, as he slipped in the pinks and reds, but every time he moved, he shifted the oils to something new. Each time, something perfect and beautiful. The darkness inside the cave shrouded his ability to see, so Andrew felt his way with his fingertips, touching the wall inside, slipping over ridges and perfect imperfections, getting hotter as he went deeper inside. "Janey." Nothing more than a whisper.

He looked back and seeing nothing in the cave behind him, he had no choice but to push ever forward, looking for escape, lost inside the gallery.

10

ANDREW OPENED HIS EYES. His dreams filled with the visions of the women in the Black Gallery, reaching out to him. To touch him. Feel him. Please his every desire. The sky above him was stark and swirling. Far above, yet right there, only inches from him. He lay there, the ground warm, wet. Lifted his arm, and looked at the slick paint on his arm. He looked up. To her.

She was made of the oil.

"Janey," he said.

She shook her head. "I should have listened," she said. Her voice was indistinct. Oozing from her like liquid. "I ..." she looked like she couldn't find the words. "I fell into a ... painting."

I know. Andrew shook his head. *I think I walked into one's vagina.* Best not bring that up. He tried to push himself to his feet, his hand sliding through the oil below him, turning grass green to straw yellow, to water blue, as he slipped like a baby deer. "Where are we?" he asked, looking out to the seas of colour around him.

"I don't know," she said. "I'm sorry. I only just got here."

"I followed you straight away. Got a cab. Tried to help ..." his voice drifted off as she threw herself into his arms. The two of them slipping together into each other's embrace, briefly becoming one as their colours conjoined and moved and changed.

She pulled back, the feeling, alien. "What are we?" she asked.

"Art," said Andrew, his voice remaining determined. He couldn't let her see him falter. Now was his time. He could fix this. Be a hero. *Yes*, he thought. *Be a hero and get the girl.* His thought flickered to her, naked, touching herself in the painting. As much a memory of that, as of her … *doing* that … before. "Okay," he said, looking from her out into the distance again. "I'll fix this." His eyes slid across the horizon, so far away, yet so close he could reach out and touch it. But when he brought his hand up, he couldn't … quite … reach it.

"What about that?" Janey said, pointing out a different direction —one that didn't feel like it had been there before. Dimensions in space, arcing and moving.

Andrew squinted into the distance. A tower, painted in black. It looked like the walls were moving and the shadows danced. "Fucking hell," he whispered. "Very creepy." He looked at her. Smiled. "Looks fine," he said, louder. He held out his hand and took hers, the two of them holding on, slipping like they were lubed until they could be lubed no more. "Come on," he said, looking up to the sky. "We need to go … before nightfall?" He scoured the sky for the sun, but saw nothing indicating it to be either day or night and perhaps something in between.

The building rose from the oil like a grandfather clock, rising from a sea of blood. The closer they got, the darker it became. The walls were wet, drooling down as gravity pulled the paint towards the ground, but some unseen artist kept pushing it back up. Janey tried to hold on to Andrew tighter, but his skin slipped uselessly beneath hers. "No," she said, trying to pull him away from it. "It's too … frightening."

Andrew looked up at the gothic architecture bleeding itself to the canvas before them, becoming one with the grass, greening to grey. "Nah," Andrew said, swallowing back the lie, "it'll be fine." He shot her a grin, glancing around the landscape looking for something—anything—else that he could head towards where he might find salvation. He saw nothing but the eternity of paint. Seeping into the sky. Blending with the ground. Archways raised in the dark building, eyebrows of surprise at their approach. Needless gargoyles sniggering in the gloom, unseen, and then painted out, like God himself was the artist, and Andrew and Janey nothing but a smear.

Andrew felt it all a little depressing, actually.

As they reached the rise to the building, Andrew could make out the doorways, giant horrifying things, capable of fitting through monsters. He shook the thought away. The only monster he planned on having to deal with, was Hampton.

That cunt.

He drew to a stop, still holding Janey. "Rest for a moment. I don't see any other buildings. This must be how we got here." The memory of what happened after the giant oil vagina was gone, nothing but wet darkness engulfing him. But this had to be it, right? "It's all fucking bollocks, though," he said. He straightened and gestured to the world around them. "I mean, drugs or something?"

Janey shook her head. "It doesn't feel *not real*."

Andrew glanced at her. "Yeah," he muttered, looking at the openings in the yawning building. He didn't want to go in there. He really, really, didn't. "The only way forward," he muttered. Another quick glance around the paint-scape and then he took her hand again. "I've got you. This is all going to be fine." He waved his arm across the hellscape like some grand gesture. "Fine," he said, again punctuating.

He took her slippery hand and led her towards the opening, a crack in the black anus of the building. There had to be a way out of this … dream … in there. This was a dream, right? Fucking nightmare, whatever. The Black Gallery. A fucking arsehole tourist spot in shit-town nowhere, and it turns out to be the vagina gateway to fucking … he looked around again. Paint Hell. Fuck it. He was taking her to a museum next time. If they ever got out of this.

No.

When. *When* they got out of this.

They approached the door, the walls flexing in and out like the building itself breathed. "Right," he said, more to himself than Janey. "Piece of cake. Walk in the park."

Fucking bollocks.

11

ANDREW SLIPPED his head around the oozing frame of the doorway leading into the cavernous hole in the landscape. He was careful not to touch the moving sides of, well, any of it. Janey behind him, her hand on his shoulder like some damsel in distress.

Yes. He was *Errol Flynning* this, rather, wasn't he?

Andrew smiled to himself. Well. Maybe next time she'd listen. He tried to keep his attention on the surrounding ... building. It was hard to think of it as a building. What with the movement and all, but it was. Definitely. Even if it *was* a hallucination. It just reminded him of something.

Inside the doorway, an opening led out to a nave, a thousand rows of black seats—pews—all facing a chancel, podium, and altar. The pews breathed as the floor rose and fell. The inside of this abomination of a church—a cathedral—a living *thing* that they had just stepped into. He squeezed her one hand, feeling her other slip in the paint of his back.

"What is it?" she said.

"It's a cathedral, I think, but something doesn't feel right."

"No shit."

He glanced back at her and smirked. "Quite." He pulled her

forward, entering the sanctity of the oil building in the landscape, changing around them. And now, once inside the cathedral, the outside seemed dark. Like the sun that never existed had crested the impossible horizon and night time had taken the painting.

He turned his attention back to the cathedral. Looking for a doorway—exit—the moving floor and walls, all matte black with an equally impossible light similar to that which had disappeared outside, replacing it there, inside. Andrew glanced up, quite the involuntary action, laying eyes on the ceiling. The ceiling of a traditional cathedral would be painted by Michelangelo or some such, but the ceiling there moved, a swirl of the past and the present and the future, rolling together. As each shape formed, the last was washed away, discarded to the side like its beauty and workmanship were a trifle, nothing more than an inconvenience. Andrew brought his eyes down the oil bleeding walls, back to the vacuous space they currently inhabited. There had to be more to *this* than just an empty church made of living blackness. There was a single door on the other side of the pews. Looked like it might have been back out, but Andrew wasn't about to take any chances in this place. The words impossible and dreadful, forefront in his mind. He knew that nothing was as it seemed.

He led Janey across. "Come on," he said, quietly, leading her down between two rows of seating, towards the other door.

"Are you sure?" she asked, her voice low.

Andrew could see the look on her face, mimicking his own worry. Her voice coloured with fear. He glanced to the pews, moving. What if they lived? What if they swallowed them? Crushed them? He looked around. There was no other way to the door. And he feared that to return to the outside would only lead them away from the inevitable. So, he continued with her, forward. "It's fine," he said. "They're just hanging out. Chilling." He wasn't even convincing himself. He pulled her until they were free of the confines of the aisles before he stopped moving. Looking to the nave of the church.

There was a smudge in the paint that looked like a shadow.

Eerie, dark. It watched them. Andrew felt a great eagerness from it, like he was going the right way. But he didn't know if he was going the right way for him, her, or *that thing*. That thing that watched.

He didn't stare. Didn't want Janey to look and see it. If it was really there, of course. She would be scared. And he needed her. Her strength. If she believed. If she believed in him, then he could do anything. "Come on," he said. "This has to be the way out."

Taking her to the door, he reached forward. The door handle, rising and falling. *It was drugs*, he said to himself. Hampton's fucking drugged them. Maybe just him. Janey might not even be with him, just a figment of his imagination. She might be there. With *him*. In that studio. Naked. Hampton eye fucking her while he splashed his … paint … up her canvas. He looked back at Janey, his fingers close to the handle, but not touching it yet. No. This was her. It was too *her* to not be her. He gently squeezed her hand and when her eyes met his, she squeezed back, gently.

"Us against them," he said.

"Always," she replied. There was a glimmer of a smile from her and in that second, he knew it *was* her.

He gripped the handle and twisted it, the pulsing door opening out to a corridor, not to the outside, as he suspected, but white. Long. Oily.

He shook his head.

Now he knew what the cathedral reminded him of.

12

"WE'RE STILL HERE," Andrew hissed as they both looked down the white corridor, painted to carry light, with three figures further down. Shadowed, but clearly, three women. *The* three women.

"Who are they? Where are we?" Janey hissed.

This was probably going to cause an argument later, but Andrew spoke, sighing as he went, "This is *the* corridor—the one that had the mannequins in before. You know," he continued, "*the* mannequins."

She nodded. "Right." She glanced back into the church. "So, are we still in The Black Gallery?"

Andrew shrugged. "Maybe. A wild trip? Inside a fucking self portrait? Who fucking knows?" He breathed slow. This fucking place. Fucking ... *ugh*.

"So, they're just mannequins?" she said, a little brighter.

"I doubt that." Andrew's memories of the things were far different to hers. He stepped forward, leading Janey through into the corridor, as the door painted itself closed behind them, some unseen brush pushing the oils over the space, filling it with white.

"What do you mean?"

He said, "You've seen the place. You must know by now that what I saw the first time was real, and that my rantings weren't the machinations of some delusional madman trying to get his wife to not *be done.*"

"The women," she whispered. "The *nakedness.*"

Andrew was dry mouthed. "Yes," he said, quietly. Waiting for the *I bet you enjoyed that* jibe.

"It wasn't your fault," she said, rather surprisingly. "I don't know what he did to cast that … spell … over me. It's all my fault."

Andrew straightened. He looked down at her looking up into his face, hers warm and smooth. "I love you," he said. Finally, seeing clearly.

"I love you too," she replied. She fired a wink at him. "What now, lover boy?"

He shot a look down the corridor. "Let's find a way outta here and blow this joint." He took her hand and led her towards the first of the mannequin women. No idea what to expect in … this … place. Women? Automatons? Monsters?

No.

The first of the women turned towards their approach, her beauty only matched by the gaping wound in her torso, a breast lolling each side of it, her fingers teasing the edge of it, like it grati-fied her to touch her wound. Stroke her gash.

You get the idea.

Andrew swallowed, walking slowly, slowing Janey in the process, getting close enough to see inside the crevice in her. Open and exposed, the cavern impossibly deeper than she was, her paint slipping within the reality around her as if she was being painted and re-painted. Her skin, herself, being molested into place by a deity that changed its mind over and again. Making her new. Old. And new again. Her hands ever present at the edges of her cleft gape, closer, the inside looked like an eternity of paint. Worlds painted on worlds, painted over the top of each other, mixed together. Bleeding together. Forged.

The mannequin's mouth gurned to a contortion of pleasure as they got closer, murmurs of orgasm coming from her lips, neither audible nor silent. Sound brushed into the world, then smeared out.

Janey pulled back on Andrew's hand, not wanting to get any closer. She held him tight, and their paint slipped together.

"It's okay," he whispered. "I've got you."

As the two of them got close, the woman bled from her torso, gushing fluids from her, weakening the strength of her paint as the fluid mixed with it, watering her colour down, paling her. Clear liquids coming from her, becoming one with the paint, like an artist's water pot. Dipping in the paint and then washing it away. "Please," the silent word drew from her, halfway painted to reality. "Fuck me," she said.

"Not today, thank you," Andrew replied as stiffly as he could. "I'm married." He pulled Janey close and started to push forward, passing the woman as best he could, like she was a busker on the underground and he had no change and the fucker was only playing yesterday over and over. He shouldered into the painting, the woman slooping around him, the two of them briefly becoming one with each other as he slipped inside her.

"Yes," she cried out, like he was some overly hung monster cock baring sex object.

"Fuck you," Janey cried out. She raised her hand to strike the painting, but Andrew stopped her.

"No," he said. "You can't be in her, too." He yanked her in front of him. Getting her safely across the front of the painting, as he tried to pull himself free. Her paint oozing out, reds and blacks, clumps and lumps inside the viscera, like clots in the paints, fetid, the smell of death coming from her as she tried to pull him in closer. Inside her.

The painting crawled over him. On him. The paint starting to mix with his own. Andrew couldn't tell if he could part himself from her. *It.* He was slowly becoming one with her. He swung out, enraged, panicked. His fists slamming into the effigy of a woman, slamming into her face, her oil slapping out like a ... fist punching a wet painting ... but instead of her face snapping back, she puddled, the flesh tones of her skin-paint parting, and the daubs becoming brain matter, the blood spraying, arterial, spattering over Andrew, Janey, and the walls, smearing over them, joining with them.

The monstrosity fell back, smearing itself against the wall, departing from Andrew and collapsing to the floor. Andrew, spinning himself away, suddenly released. The wall streaked with oil, reds and blacks. Andrew grabbed Janey and started running. Down the corridor. "Come on," he blurted. *"Fuck."*

They headed towards the next of the two, already turning to greet them. The woman having a proboscis the size of a baby's arm between its legs, the shape of it changing, and curling, as if whoever ran this show thought that the crevice on the last mannequin hadn't satisfied him, so perhaps *this* would.

There was a baby's face on the end of it, painted into creation. It screamed out to Janey first, like her foul offspring, crying for mother's milk, before it recoiled, like it remembered it didn't like chicks or something, changing its mind and turning to face Andrew, a baby oil face screaming in wet desire.

Andrew glanced back, the thought of retreat suddenly very, very, viable. But he knew they had to push on. They had to face whatever The Black Gallery threw at them. He didn't know why. He just *knew.*

The baby-faced penis suddenly jerked forward, pulling the painted mannequin woman nearly from her feet, snaking like an anaconda, the paint of it, scarring the corridor floor as it pulled its colour over the layers of white oil. Andrew glanced back again. The first one was fixing itself, or something was fixing it. Paint rolling over the wounds in its head, the pooling paint from the hole being pushed back into the thing's gash, like someone trying to push water uphill.

Andrew released Janey, grabbing the baby-faced penis in his hand like a business man's two-handed shake. That over the top, underneath, power handshake. Twisting and twirling the things face before it could grab him with its penis-faced mouth and start to paint itself into him. Dosey doe-ing his partner (taking it by the face) he catapulted himself. Slingshot around the mannequin woman and fired her at the first one as it got to its feet, reimagined into the corridor. Its aching torso maw salaciously drooling at the thought of possessing Andrew. *Of consuming his oil.*

The two monsters slooshed together like two artist's palettes being banged together by a raucous uncontrolled child. Paint slipping aside the corridor's white, smearing together with the pinks and yellows, reds, biles ... all becoming a single shade of brown, like all paints do when they inevitably merge into oneness.

Looked a bit like shit, to be honest.

The final of the three lady mannequin harlot things turned, screeching out a loud, horrid, cry as it bore witness to the plunder of its coven's colours. Andrew grabbing Janey by the hand, and rushed towards the creature.

It pushed its own paint, hands and fingers into itself. Changing the look of itself to something else. The sex of the mannequin, rebooted to that of a creature, spawned of the imagination of something most foul. The visage grew as it moved itself outward, becoming larger, changing colour and thickness. New paint is coming from nowhere, the beauty of the pinks, the red of its sex, becoming a dark rouge, inclement to the eye. The form bringing with it the disgusting stench of rotting food. The form of a woman returned as that of a beast; tall, hunched, rippling with muscle, distorted from human to some unspeakable creation. A tongue licked out of its black and darkened maw, teeth, yellow and extended, chomping down as it could already savour the taste of the two of them.

Andrew tried to pull Janey forward, but she stopped him. "No," she said. "We have to turn back."

Andrew looked. The corridor clear of obstacles apart from the sticky mess that used to be those painted lady mannequins. It was true, the way back was safest, but that would lead to the cathedral again, and that shadow, watching. At best, back out into the endless painted landscape. The nothingness where they awoke together.

"No," he said, standing firm. "*We* can do this." His eyes met hers. "I believe in us. You. We can beat fucking Hampton and his stupid pissing gallery." He looked up at the ceiling before bellowing, "You hear me, Hampton? Your art *sucks balls.*"

Janey let out a shy giggle, before covering her mouth, her eyes returning to the monstrosity in the hallway.

It wasn't approaching them. It stood waiting, like a guard dog told to heel. Protect the door.

"Look," she said, the creature standing there, rooted to the spot it begun on.

"I know," he whispered. "It's still the mannequin it always was … stuck on the spot. At least, until we're closer."

"I don't understand," she whispered.

"Neither do I." He pulled her around behind him and stepped toward the thing. It stood, head and shoulders over him, twice as wide, a penis hanging limp between its legs as long as Andrew's arm. Pointing, Andrew shouted, "Now I say," his finger flickered to the door. "We're going through and there is nothing—*nothing, you hear me*—that you can do about it." He stepped a single, slow step forward. Raised his eyebrows.

He wondered where Janey had parked when she arrived for her *done-ing.* Hoped she had put long enough on the ticket. Probably didn't have enough coins. Andrew shook his head. What the fuck was he thinking?

He stepped forward again, and the creature cried out. Its bellow filling the emptiness of the corridor, harsh and abrasive to the ear. It raised its huge hands, fisted claws digging into the paint of its own palms, causing them to bleed out like stigmata.

It punched a fist into the wall, the white of that sticking syrupy to the creature's own colour, blending in, and disappearing as its skin rippled and rolled. Over painting itself, over, and over. Paint rolling like the ocean, tidal and unending.

Andrew dropped Janey's hand, taking broad steps towards the creature, and raising his foot. Swift kick in the gonads always did away with the biggest bullies in the playground, eh? He contacted with the creature, but instead of recoiling away, the creature's elongated love sausage snaked out to his leg; the paint mixing betwixt them; it curling around him. Touching him. Taking him. His foot being sucked into the ball-sack of the creature, its appendage holding him tight. Tighter. Like a python, squeezing the life out of him. Pulling him from his feet.

"Run, Janey," Andrew screamed. "The door. Go. Now." He was dragged from his feet, pulled toward the creature like an octopus, lifted from the wet white of the floor, leaving a snail trail of pale on his torso, the white taking his own colour. Turning his saturation down to nothing.

Janey started to him. Desperate to help.

"No," Andrew screamed. He held his hand out, pulled up by the foot, upside down, his paint rushing to his head. "Go. Please."

Janey twisted mid-run, seeking a door handle with her grasping fingers. The creature's attention taken by her.

"Look at me, you son of a bitch," Andrew screamed.

And the creature did.

13

THE LAST THING Andrew saw was Janey dragging the door of the corridor open, lurching through into the darkness beyond, before the coil of the creature's sex dropped him back to the floor. The white paint spattering wetly to his face, the stink of oil, pungent, as it curled its grotesque snake towards his mouth.

Andrew tried to pull his foot free from the thing's torso as it suckled on his foot like a baby at its mother's teat. Holding him. Tight and firm. "Fuck you," he snapped out, embittered. "Fuck you, Hampton."

The wild slipping organ probed to his mouth and pushed his lips open. Andrew tried to stop it. His mouth clenched tight as the phallus pushed against him. His hands around it, trying to choke it, push it away. It slipped its wet tip between his lips. His teeth clamped firmly shut, pushed open, as it invaded his mouth. The taste of oil. The paint. Sticky, sickly sweet, as it rolled over his tongue. Andrew, breathing through his nose, his eyes darting back and forth, looking for some release, as the creature brayed its head back in ecstasy, Andrew's mouth taking its girth.

He could feel the paint slipping down inside him, passing his gag reflex, making his stomach turn and twist, feeling the bile coming up to greet the snake inside him, pushing his paint around, remaking his insides.

He felt it recoil as his puke reached the glans of the creature, acidic and burning, washing away the top layer of the creature's paint, a rice pudding skin on the oil. The creature snarled at him, as Andrew attempted a smile, his maw held open by the thing's huge penis. Andrew pushed himself back, holding it at bay, pushing his free foot against the painted flesh next to his partially absorbed foot. Pushing himself away from the creature, his eyes meeting its, as its cock slipped back, fought back by the rising acid reflux in his throat.

The phallus, out, puke drooling out of Andrew's gob, onto his chin. The creature released his foot and Andrew finally managed to pull back. "Yeah," he said, like he'd won some victory. "You don't like that, do you?" Andrew wiped the puke paint from his chin with the back of his forearm, the paint from his clothes, mixing with puke and skin tones.

The creature cried, cradling its appendage, white, bleached by the contents of Andrew's rancid guts. Hurt by his bile.

He pushed himself to his feet. "Fucking paint monsters," he said, like it was an everyday occurrence. Andrew turned and ran for the door, left open, into the darkness.

To Janey.

14

THE MACHINE THRUST itself into the mannequin woman, her paint mixing with its own, the two of them becoming one. Wet, viscous paints mixing together inside the woman's torso, she cried out in pleasure, then in pain, her slippery organs moved and shuffled by its gargantuan girth, thrusting deep within her cavernous body, open, gaping. Bloody paint mess squirted out of her, as the machine pushed into her, flooding it out over her torso, up to her face, deep waters created, flowing. Her look was that of perfect desire, lust. Love. Then turning to pain as the machine pulled back, hate, horror, as it withdrew its phallus from her. Bent in agony at losing it—this part of her.

Andrew's face contorted as the woman screamed out orgasmic pleasure at the thing defiling her, his eyes dropping to Janey on the other side of the room. She was staring, her mouth gaping open, her fingers gently on her face as she tried to cover her mouth, but had forgotten where it truly was.

Andrew dashed to her side, taking her face in his shoulder. "Don't look, my love," he said. Pulling her close. "It's … not real," he whispered. "It can't be." He was trying to persuade himself, as much as her. He knew that.

He just hoped that she didn't.

"Andrew," she wept into his paint. "Where are we ... what's happening?"

He shook his head. "I don't know. But I'll fix it." He gently pushed her from his embrace, looking down into her eyes. "I promise." His smile small, but reassuring.

She nodded, brushing the tears into her flesh, beading at first, then the oil absorbing the water.

He took her hand, giving the fucking machine a single glance, before turning away. The woman riding it, recoiling in pleasure from its touch. Unable to take more, and more, and more. He drove the vision from his head and pulled Janey to the door.

The next room. Empty. Straight across and out. Into the room with the living painting. The one that repainted itself. The one that touched him. He dreaded what they might see next.

Pushing the door open, he stepped through, the paint of the walls making it look like they'd stepped into a Rubens. The walls filled with bookshelves, hued and surreal looking. Yet everything looked like everything else, painted into reality. The chair in the centre of the room stood, the table, both oozing two dimensions, yet as they crossed the space, it became liminal, the flattened objects gaining depth, the sensation sickening, like moving between realities. There was coffee on the table. The room smelt of paint and mince pie, a lurid sickly, smell. Manufacturing plants and Christmas. The steam from the mug being stirred about by some unseen brush ... the white of it painted in, moved, and then being absorbed into the canvas behind it.

Andrew swallowed back the sickness still in his throat, able to taste the salty paint of the last thing he had in there. Squeezing Janey's hand, reassuring her.

"I don't understand," she said.

"I don't think you're supposed to," he replied, choking back the seasickness the room gave him, a swirling sensation. Andrew knew that the room had more to offer, but not what that was going to be. He jumped, the quiet of the room broken by the door opening from the floor in the far corner of the room. He pulled Janey around behind him. Held her there. Not knowing.

The brilliance of the light behind the door glistened on the wet paint of the flat surfaces, the woman beyond stepping out. She was painted as a nude this time. Utterly stunning … more perfect than the light that surrounded her. The room suddenly flooded with the cooling breeze of whatever was beyond that door. Somewhere Andrew had never even thought of. He watched her step out into the room with suspicion. Knowing that Janey was going to be there behind him, looking at her. Probably judging his want of her against this visage that he had seen before. The one that had touched him. He scoffed. She had nothing to worry about there.

Fucking drop dead gorgeous, Janey was. Always would be.

He still had her hand, pulling her tight in behind him. Reassuring her, that he might be looking at this … image of desire … but he was only thinking of her. She whispered, *I love you*, in his ear.

He thought about replying something cool. Something *Han Solo* like. But decided on, "I love you, too."

The two of them watched as the woman entered the room. She came to them slowly, like an apparition, until she was almost close enough to touch. *Almost.* Her breasts hung, tight and pert, but large. Her body curved like a model in the seventies. Andrew could feel his body respond. He knew that she'd been painted to please him. Like this fucking place could read his mind.

"She looks like me," Janey said, quietly. The observation borne from confusion.

Andrew looked again. She *did*. She wasn't painted to meet his desires. *Or she was*. But his desire was his wife. It *was* her body.

"I don't …" she said.

Andrew shook his head, pulling his eyes from the woman as she stared at him. Tempting him. He knew that was what she was doing. She was trying to lure him. He didn't understand though … what did the painting think it could offer him that she couldn't already? The oil moved as she slowly gyrated, hips swaying, in seduction. Andrew looked around her to the door. The one back to the beginning. There, beyond the mince pie coffee. "We need to get out of here," he said.

Then he lunged.

He thrust himself forward, his elbow going into the sexy oil woman, all *looking like his wife*, out to the coffee table, which he kicked, mince pie coffee flinging itself into the gleaming silken oil, drooling off it like cum on a porn star. The table scattered to the floor, the brown of its legs smearing on the red of the carpet, an orange, then back to red, as the painting absorbed it, no longer required in the landscape. Andrew held Janey with one hand, brushing down the whore's paint from his shoulder. Trying to be cool. He glanced at her, worried that this might be all too much, and that she might ...

... not want to love him anymore.

Having seen into his mind. His psyche.

But she looked determined. Egged on by his bravado. His perceived bravado, anyway. He was just hoping his trousers weren't turning brown. "Enough of this bullshit," he scowled, reaching the door to the room beyond. In the gallery, this was the reception room. Here ...

He pushed it open, almost falling into the room beyond.

A quick look around. The walls ... real. Matte black. He looked back to Janey. She was re-made of flesh. A look down at himself. As was he. The two of them were back in The Black Gallery. Smeared in oil paint.

He held her tight. Feeling the heat of her skin on his. Her realness.

"Where are we?" she asked. "Are we ...?"

He looked at the walls, the doors, the sofa. It all looked like they were back in The Black Gallery, but Andrew was nobody's fool. "Hampton," he called. "Show yourself. Explain yourself."

The unmistakeable sound of Hampton filled the room, a deep yet short laugh, as the walls started to move again, an all too familiar motion, breathing, back and forth slowly. "And there was me thinking I deceived you." From inside him, his voice was booming and ominous.

"You'll never fool me," Andrew shouted back. "How do we get out of this place?" He glanced to Janey, making sure she was still on his side, clung to him like a damsel.

"I believe in you," she said.

Andrew nodded. Good. He believed in her, too. Her trust in him was still unbroken. He needed that. He needed her to believe in him. Nothing without her. He never had been. She was his rock. His beginning. His everything.

"Hampton," he cried out. "End this."

The door that led to the street clicked open. Andrew couldn't see any sunlight beyond. Another trick, no doubt. The Black Gallery leading them forward to some other horrific visage. He stepped across the room, leading Janey, and as they got closer to the door, he could see that there was darkness beyond it.

Andrew looked through.

The cathedral beyond.

Back to the beginning of where they were only a while ago. "What is this, Hampton?"

"All journeys must have a trial, Andrew," he responded, the floor moving in time with his speech, the room cradling them as it breathed.

"God damn it," Andrew huffed. "Do we get photos on this ride?"

The floor moved, grumbling.

15

ANDREW HELD JANEY'S HAND, the two of them watching the shadow that still stood at the altar, at the front of the cathedral. "Hampton," Andrew muttered.

Janey tugged on his arm a little. Wanting to leave, obviously.

He wanted to leave, too.

No doubt.

The smear on the cathedral beckoned them forward. Andrew, standing his ground. But Janey moved, like she was entranced by it. *Him*. Fucking Hampton again. She released his hand and pulled away from him. Almost floating across the room to *him*. Her fingers reaching out toward the artist's shadow.

"Janey," Andrew hissed. "Don't. It's a trick."

She ignored him. Taken entirely by Hampton's pull, his lure.

Then the doors at the end of the Cathedral, the opposite end to Hampton, clicked, swinging open. Daylight beyond, illuminating the inside of the cathedral like the fires of hell, spawning in the darkness. Andrew looked from the light to the darkness, Hampton's shadow made stronger by the light. Deeper. Thicker.

Darker.

Janey, now with him. Stood like a bride at the end of the church, waiting to take her husband.

"Go," Hampton said. The walls of the building speaking. "You may leave and be free."

"Janey," Andrew called back. She didn't respond, taken by whatever wicked spell he had cast over her.

"Leave." The walls of the cathedral breathed the word out. "Go now."

Andrew turned. The doors of the cathedral are so close to him. Janey so far. Her mind gone. Taken by the artist. His temptation. He stepped towards the doors, looking out. Reality beyond. He could see the street. The warmth of the sun drying the oil on his skin. *Reality*, he thought. It was true. It *was* the way out.

He reached the door, walking slowly, his feet moving without him even noticing. Like he, too, was floating.

His hand, on the handle of the door. Feeling it. Not slippery and wet, but *real* … tangible. A thing. He looked back to Janey, stood, admiring the man. The wrong man. His eyes returning to the street outside. People out there. Walking by. He didn't even call out. He knew that they wouldn't hear. Not while he was in there. Inside the Gallery. Inside the art. Fresh air blew in his face. The light smell of salt that all seaside towns had in the air. A freshness. The sound of the herring gulls screeching in the distance. Probably attacking someone for chips.

"When the door closes," the cathedral drawled the words out, "the lock will cross forever." It—*he*—let the ominous words hang in the oil before continuing. "Whether you choose to be inside me … or out."

Andrew touched the lock, his fingers slipping around it. He turned, letting the handle go. Releasing the door. "I want my wife back."

Hampton released a long laugh. "Oh, dear Andrew."

The whole cathedral felt like it moved, the paint sliding as some unseen force made Andrew brace, stopping himself from being pushed backwards.

The door slammed behind him.

He glanced back, holding himself steadfast against Hampton's wont. "Fuck you, old man," he screamed.

The hall fell silent, his voice echoing around as the force stopped. Andrew standing back, upright, no longer braced. He breathed deep. The smell of oil in every lungful. He was hot. It felt hotter in there now, like the door closing off the outside was claustrophobic. He walked to the pews and started down towards the front of the cathedral. His eyes moving between Janey and Hampton. The old man's face now partially visible inside the shadow, his cheeks, glinting as the light bounced from his paint, smearing and smudging, a smile on his face, teeth white in the darkness.

"Good," he said. "I have you both."

Andrew stopped. Feet from the two of them. "What the fuck could you possibly want with us?" He shook his head, his eyes darting around, looking for something to attack Hampton with. Something to rearrange his paint job.

Hampton grinned. "I want your wife's heart and soul."

Andrew's eyes fell on Janey. She was staring at Hampton. Into him. She looked like an adoring puppy. Under some sort of spell. There was no way it was actually her. Not like that. She loved *him*. He *knew* that. "Well, you can't have her." Andrew lunged forward, his hands out in front of him, reaching for Hampton, to grab him. Tackle him to the ground.

Actually, that was about as far as he'd gotten with this plan. Some years ago, back in his old school days, he'd gotten into a rumble or two, a bit a pushing in the changing room. Flicking towels, that sort of thing. But in all actuality, he'd never been much of a hands-on fighter. He'd always talked his way around the actual fights long before he'd gotten to the fist stage, mostly claiming that *fighting never solved anything*. Which wasn't true, was it? Fighting tended to solve lots of things. Like this. This was probably going to be solved by fighting, because what other choice does he have? Locked in some oil slicked cathedral painted into some impossible landscape, full of shadow people and strangely erotic malformed mannequin ladies.

No, the reason he'd always talked his way out of fighting was that he was, deep down, afraid of getting smacked in the chops.

But this seemed all a bit beyond that now. So, he'd decided to take the Neanderthal way out. And threw himself into Hamptons smudged likeness.

16

ANDREW'S FIST smooshed into the paint of Hampton's face ... thing. He stumbled back, roaring out in anger, stumbling up the steps towards a randomly placed lectern. Tumbling, falling over his own paint. His features were already a weird fucking blur, and after Andrew had managed to lay his hand into his face, it looked somehow *more* disfigured. Andrew stood, admiring his work. Not too shabby for a fucking coward. *Pacifist,* he berated himself in his head. *Pacifist.*

He was still congratulating himself when Hampton started to change.

From within the shadows of his ... body? Torso? Sort-of-cloaky-thing? A giant hand painted itself into being, huge boned, gnarled, red paints dripping from its elongated nails. It rose from the centre of the ... Hampton thing ... up and out like an unnameable eldritch creature, birthing from within him.

Andrew stepped back. "Blimey," he said.

From within Hampton came another hand, rising up, one each planting itself down on the floor of the cathedral, palm down and pushing itself out of his vacuous space, like a full-grown man, creeping from a very sore vagina. It rose out, giant head squeezing through the hole that used to be Hampton. Now, nothing more than a giant birthing canal. The horned creature was painted with what Andrew considered to be far too much red, a long snarling face, half man, half badger, half demon, part horse, part actual insides on the outside. It crawled out of the mess of Hampton paint, standing over eight feet tall, on steps over Andrew, increasing its height still further. Oil running from its oversized maw, standing betwixt the two of them, its whole being bobbing as it breathed air in like a one hundred and ten metre hurdler, having just broken the world record…

Andrew looked down at his slight pot-belly.

He took in a deep breath, straightening his back. "That all you got?" he shouted up at the face of the demon.

The thing snorted. It pointed at Janey, turning its hand and curling its finger, beckoning her to it.

And she obeyed without a word or question.

Janey walked to its side, her head only just over the height of its hips, as she smeared her own paint over it. *His.* Andrew knew Hampton was still in there somewhere. Her hands writhing up, over the creature's cock. Making it hard. All the while, he stared at Andrew, like he was waiting. Waiting for Andrew to do something.

Taunting him.

Andrew watched the creature, excited at his wife's touch. His cock, huge and engorged. *Come on*, he thought to himself, *man up*. "I say," he bellowed, pointing at the Hampton demon. "This is between you and me."

"I *shall* take a heart." The words crawled from the creature's mouth. He, it, them, this *thing* looked at Janey. "And a body, it appears." He snorted, his muscular frame tightening as he enjoyed the intense sexual awakening caused by Janey, her hands deft, her lips touching his torso now. His paint on her beautiful mouth. Dirtied by his paint. She was pushing against his thigh, fucking his leg like a dog as she pleased him.

Andrew felt sick. His stomach turned, watching his wife, helplessly helping this … thing … towards orgasm.

No. Not this time, Satan. Andrew stepped in front of the creature. He reached up, slipping his fingers inside his shirt, and pulling it open, tearing it like he was God damned Superman. Baring his chest. He let the shirt hang, as he pushed his fingers against his skin, his paint. The tips sliding into his chest, through the paint, his oil pooling out of him, through his canvas.

Andrew screamed a perfect scream of pain and torment.

With his fingers inside his body, he pulled. Harder than he had ever pulled before, drawing his hands away from each other like he was pulling a Christmas cracker alone, his chest opening, red paint spitting out of the wound as his canvas cracked open, the sound of nuts being brutalised echoing around the cathedral hall. His painted bones breaking.

His chest opened, the cavity spilling blood over his clothes, his paint pooling deeply on the floor, his lungs inflating and deflating, fast and hard, as he breathed, raked in suffering. He reached in and grasped his painted heart in his fist. Feeling the muscle pulsate in his grip, he yanked it from his body. Holding it, beating, to the creature.

"Take mine," he screamed. "Let my wife go."

The creature looked stunned. Just for a moment, as he stood there, offering his still beating heart forward. A gift. To release his Janey.

The spell faltered, and Janey staggered back. A look of horror painted her face, realising her touches had caused this … Eiffel Tower before her. She recoiled. Her paint yellowing, before she looked to Andrew, his heart beating.

Only for her.

Andrew looked at her. "Come on, Babe. Let's blow this joint." The pain rising over every inch of Andrew's body. The impossible, possible, as he pushed the heart back into the paint, smearing his fingers into the red, reconnecting it to the rest of his slick and wet insides. Janey ran to him, they took each other's hands, turning, running to the door, like lovers on a beach in a shit romance film. Or Rocky and Apollo. Tom and Val.

"The door remains locked forever, Andrew," the Hampton demon spoke, angered, a low growl running under every word.

Janey looked to Andrew; her belief unbroken.

Andrew reached the door first, his hand slipping as he gripped the door handle, turning it.

The door opening.

"What?" the demon bellowed, its anger filling the void of the cathedral.

Andrew guided Janey through, out into the bright sunlight beyond. He pulled the object that he'd jammed in the lock of the door, stopping it from locking shut, holding it up to the creature, sunlight bouncing from the golden metal. "Tesco trolley pound coin, motherfucker," Andrew shouted, thrusting it back in his painted trousers, because he was definitely going to stop and pick up a bottle of something stronger than cola on the way home.

"No," the creature screamed, the walls of the cathedral shuddering in the wake of the cry, the paint dancing and lurching. Spasms as the reality in the gallery broke.

17

ANDREW STAGGERED TO THE PAVEMENT, Janey taking him in her arms as the doors to The Black Gallery closed behind them. Her fingers slipped into his paint on his chest, trying to sooth him. The two of them stumbling out into the road.

He reached up and touched his chest, as the pain subsided, his body complete again. The red paint dripping from him, drying under his fingers, over his clothes torn and ripped. He took Janey in his arms, half naked, pulling her close and kissing her deeply.

"Oh, Andrew," she said. "You saved me."

His heart beat hard—in his chest—his cock twitched—in his trousers—, "Only for you," he whispered, plunging his tongue in between her lips, tasting her wetness … *human* wetness. The taste of oil and paint gone from his mouth.

"Gross," said some kid on the path. Little fucker.

The two of them parted, Andrew smiling. "So where did you park?" he asked.

She started laughing, the fear, pain, running away like brushes in water, losing their dirt. "Only down the road."

Andrew took her hand, and they stepped up onto the path on the other side of the road. Looking to the gallery. He led her away. Up, towards the car. "So, maybe next time ... the cinema?"

"Yes," she said. "I don't think I want anyone to do me, apart from you."

Andrew looked into her eyes as they walked, people giving them a wide berth. Andrew, half dressed and covered in paint. "I love you," he said.

"I love you, too," she replied. "How do we get like that sometimes?" She giggled.

Andrew shook his head, a last glance back to the gallery as he pulled the car door open for her, holding it. "Hungry?" he asked. "We could go to the drive thru."

"Sounds great."

Hampton watched from the shadows in the Gallery. He watched the two of them climb in the car. Andrew's heart renewed with love for his wife. A love that had never left.

It just needed a nudge.

ABOUT THE EDITOR / PUBLISHER

Dawn Shea is an author and half of the publishing team over at D&T Publishing. She lives with her family in Mississippi. Always an avid horror lover, she has moved forward with her dreams of writing and publishing those things she loves so much.

D&T Previously published material:
    ABC's of Terror
    After the Kool-Aid is Gone

Follow her author page on Amazon for all publications she is featured in.
    Follow D&T Publishing at the following locations:
    Website
    Facebook: Page / Group
    Or email us here: dandtpublishing20@gmail.com

ASH ERICMORE

Ash Ericmore lives in Kent in England. By the seaside. He rarely leaves the house. A hermit by any other name, he lives on a council estate.

Hiding from everyone.

Seen once in shadow on a wildlife documentary, many dubious articles have been offered in attempts to prove the existence of Ericmore, including anecdotal claims of observations as well as dubious video and audio recordings, photographs, and casts of his monstrous footprints.

He is founder of the Ericmorean Church of Splatterology.

He can rarely identify an arse from an elbow.

You can find him at www.ashericmore.com.

The Black Gallery by Ash Ericmore

Cover by Ash Ericmore

Edited by Tasha Schiedel

Formatting by J.Z. Foster

The Black Gallery